The Ski Slope Mystery

Nancy pushed off and glided down the hill. As she reached the bottom, she aimed the tips of her skis together to make a wedge. It was hard to keep her feet pointed the right way, but she did it. She stopped perfectly and smiled.

Then she heard a scream.

Nancy twisted around, being careful not to cross her skis.

George was speeding down the hill right behind Bess.

"Look out, Bess!" George screamed. "I can't stop!"

The Nancy Drew Notebooks

Available from MINSTREL Books

THE NANCY DREW NOTEBOOKS® #16

THE SKI SLOPE MYSTERY

CAROLYN KEENE

Illustrated by Anthony Accardo

A MINSTREL® BOOK

PUBLISHED BY POCKET BOOKS

New York   London   Toronto   Sydney   Tokyo   Singapore

A MINSTREL PAPERBACK *Original*

 A Minstrel Book published by
POCKET BOOKS, a division of Simon & Schuster Inc.
1230 Avenue of the Americas, New York, NY 10020

Copyright © 1997 by Simon & Schuster Inc.
Produced by Mega-Books, Inc.

ISBN: 0-671-56860-4

First Minstrel Books printing January 1997

10 9 8 7 6 5 4 3 2 1

Cover art by Aleta Jenks

Printed in the U.S.A.

1

Hot Fudge
and Cold Snow

Race you to the hot fudge," George Fayne said to her cousin Bess Marvin.

"No way." Bess pushed her blond hair behind her ear and picked up her dish of chocolate ice cream. "I don't want hot fudge today. I'm having caramel."

Eight-year-old Nancy Drew smiled as she sprinkled chopped nuts over her strawberry ice cream. The three best friends were at a make-your-own-sundae party at the Snowshoe Mountain Ski Lodge.

1

Nancy's father had brought Nancy, Bess, and George to the resort for a three-day weekend. The girls were going to take skiing lessons at the Snowshoe Lodge ski school. The school had classes for everyone, from beginners to experts.

"I still can't believe we're really here," Nancy said to her friends. She glanced around the large, wood-paneled dining room. All around her, people were helping themselves to ice cream and toppings. Outside the window, snow was falling gently as the sun set behind the tall peak of Snowshoe Mountain. "I've always wanted to learn to ski."

"Me, too," Bess said.

"You'll love it," George promised. George liked all kinds of sports. She had been skiing a few times before.

The girls walked across the crowded room to the table where Mr. Drew was drinking coffee. "Do you think all these people are here for ski school?" Nancy asked her father as they sat down.

"I hope not," George said. "I want to spend the weekend skiing, not waiting in line."

"Don't worry, George." Mr. Drew smiled. "I'm sure you'll be able to do all the skiing you want."

"That's right," Bess said. "Your lucky necklace won't let you get stuck in line."

George scooped up a bite of her hot-fudge sundae and nodded.

"You mean the necklace your parents just gave you?" Nancy asked.

George swallowed her ice cream. Then she reached up and touched the pair of little silver skis hanging from a velvet ribbon around her neck. "It's my good-luck charm."

"It's great," Nancy said, looking at the tiny skis.

"Look, girls," Mr. Drew said, nodding toward the small stage at one end of the room. "They're going to make an announcement."

The girls turned and saw a man with short, sandy hair stepping up to a microphone on the stage. "May I have your attention, please?" he asked.

Nancy, Bess, and George stopped talking. But the two boys at the next table weren't paying attention to the man. They kept laughing loudly. One of them picked up a spoonful of ice cream and flipped it at the other.

The second boy leaned to the side, and the ice cream went flying past him—straight toward Bess!

Bess saw it coming just in time and ducked. The ice cream landed on the floor behind her.

"You creeps! You almost got ice cream on my sweater!" Bess cried.

The boys stared at her. They looked exactly alike. Even their clothes were the same. The only way to tell them apart was by the hot-fudge mustache one of them had on his face.

"Look, they're twins," Nancy said.

"Twin creeps, you mean," Bess said, frowning at the boys.

The boy with the fudge mustache stuck out his tongue. His brother

picked up another spoonful of ice cream and aimed it at Bess.

"Don't even think about it," Bess warned.

Mr. Drew turned and saw what was happening. "That's enough, boys," he said.

Both twins turned and faced the stage.

"I want to welcome everyone to Snowshoe Mountain," the man on the stage said. "I'm Bob Murray, the director of the ski school. How many of you are here for our ski school weekend?"

A lot of people waved their hands and cheered, including Nancy and Bess. George put two fingers in her mouth and whistled.

Bob Murray smiled. "I know you'll all have a great time and learn a lot. Now I'd like to introduce our instructors."

The ski instructors all wore black ski pants and bright red jackets.

"I love their outfits," Bess said. "They're almost as cute as my new pink ski jacket and hat." Her jacket was hanging on the back of her chair, with the pink hat tucked into the pocket.

"When you've finished eating, feel free to explore the rest of the lodge," Bob Murray said. "There's a game room across the hall, and a fireplace in the lounge. I hope everyone has a great weekend!"

"Let's go check out the game room," Nancy said to her friends. "Can we, Dad?"

"Okay," her father said. "I'll come to get you in a little while."

Nancy, Bess, and George quickly slurped down the rest of their ice cream. They picked up their jackets and hurried across the hall and into the game room.

"Looks like they're showing some cool skiing videos." George pointed to a big-screen television by the windows.

"Hey, maybe they have Star Quest," Nancy said when she saw the row of video games along the wall. The game was based on one of Nancy's favorite movies. "Let's go see."

As the girls headed toward the games, Nancy heard the sound of running footsteps. Then someone pushed Bess—hard.

She stumbled and almost fell into a table. Nancy grabbed her arm at the last minute.

"Bess, are you okay?" Nancy asked.

"My new ski hat," Bess cried. "Those twins just grabbed it out of my pocket!"

2

Double Trouble

Hat, hat, who's got the hat?" the twins chanted. They were standing behind Nancy and her friends. The twin holding Bess's new hat threw it into the air.

"Give it back!" Bess shrieked. She grabbed for the hat.

The other twin got it first. "Pink stinks, pink stinks." He threw the hat, and his brother reached forward to catch it.

George jumped up and caught the hat before the first twin reached it. *"Twins* stink," she said to the boys.

The twins stuck out their tongues

and laughed. Then they ran past the girls to the video games.

"Thanks, George," Bess said, stuffing the hat back into her pocket.

"Tim and Tom are such creeps," a girl's voice said.

Nancy turned and saw a girl about their own age standing in the doorway to the game room. She had short, smooth black hair and green eyes.

"Do you know them?" Nancy asked.

"They were in the beginners' class with me last year." The girl walked over to where Nancy, Bess, and George were standing. "They were always getting in trouble."

"*Double* trouble, I bet," George said.

The girl looked at George. "I like your necklace," she said.

George touched the tiny silver skis. "Thanks. It's my new good-luck charm. I won't ski without it."

"Are you a good skier?" the girl asked.

George shrugged. "I've only been skiing a few times. But I like it. I can't wait for ski school to start."

"I'll be in ski school, too," the girl said. "My name is Kelly Allen." Just then a girl with two long brown braids came into the game room and stood beside Kelly. "This is my little sister, Jennifer," Kelly said.

"Hi," Jennifer said, smiling.

Nancy smiled back. "Hi. I'm Nancy, and these are my friends Bess and George."

"Come on, let's watch the ski video," Kelly said. She led the way over to the big couch across from the TV.

As the girls sat down, Nancy looked at the skier on the screen. He was skiing around some orange flags. "I don't think I can do that yet," she said.

Jennifer laughed. "Me, either. I'm a beginner. I didn't get to come with Kelly last year because I had the flu."

"Bess and I are beginners, too," Nancy said. "Maybe we'll be in the same class."

"What about you, George?" Kelly asked. "Which level are you in?"

"Intermediate," George said, her eyes glued to the skier on the screen. He was gliding down a wide mountain trail, swooping back and forth to avoid rocks and trees.

"Me, too," Kelly said. "Every year there's a contest to choose the best skiers in each class. This year I know I'm going to win the award for best skier in my group."

"Who cares about winning a stupid skiing contest," a boy's voice said loudly.

The girls turned as a boy walked up to them. He had short black hair that stuck straight up.

"Skiing is *so* dumb," the boy said.

"It is not!" George said angrily.

The boy scowled at George. "Is, too."

"If you think skiing is dumb, why are you here?" Bess asked.

"My parents made me come," he said.

"Will," a woman called from the doorway.

"Coming, Mom!" the boy yelled. He stomped away without saying goodbye.

"There are *a lot* of creepy boys around this lodge," Bess said.

"He's probably just afraid to ski." George touched her necklace. "Maybe he needs a good-luck charm like mine."

"Does that really bring you luck?" Kelly asked. "Can I try it on?"

George didn't move for a moment. Nancy could tell she didn't want to take off her silver skis. But George untied the velvet ribbon and handed the necklace to Kelly anyway.

"Thanks." Kelly tied the ribbon around her own neck. "Maybe wearing it for a minute will bring me luck, too."

Nancy saw her father come into the room. "Time to go, girls," he called.

Nancy, Bess, and George put on their jackets. They said goodbye to Kelly and Jennifer and started to follow Mr. Drew out of the room.

"Oops! I almost forgot my necklace," George said.

Kelly took off the necklace. "Do you want me to tie it on for you?"

George nodded and pushed her dark curls out of the way. She smiled and touched the silver skis when they were back in place.

Bess, George, and Nancy followed Nancy's father out of the lodge and into the cold, starry night. So did Jennifer and Kelly.

"Bye!" Jennifer called from the doorway of the lodge.

Nancy turned and waved to her new friends. Jennifer waved back. But Kelly didn't see Nancy. She was busy looking at the glistening snow.

"I hope it's not this cold tomorrow," Bess said. She pulled on her pink hat.

"I don't care how cold it is," Nancy said, swishing her boots in the snow on the path. "We're going to have fun!"

It only took a few minutes to get to the apartment they were staying in for the weekend. From the living room window they could see the brightly colored gondola cars. Each day the gondolas carried skiers to the restaurant at the very top of the mountain.

It was chilly inside the apartment. Nancy quickly changed into her warm flannel nightgown and brushed her teeth. The bedroom she was sharing with Bess and George had two sets of bunk beds. She jumped into the lower bunk of one of the beds and snuggled under a cozy yellow- and white-striped comforter.

Bess came out of the bathroom and hopped into the other lower bunk. "Brrr," she said. "Hurry up and brush your teeth, George. Then you can tell us what skiing is like before we go to sleep."

"I'll be right out," George promised, rushing into the bathroom.

"I wish Chip was here," Nancy said. "She could keep my feet warm."

Chip was Nancy's Labrador retriever puppy. Her full name was Chocolate Chip because she was a chocolate brown color.

Suddenly George came racing out of

the bathroom with toothpaste foam around her mouth. She was waving her toothbrush.

"George, what's wrong?" Nancy asked.

"My necklace!" George cried. "It's gone!"

3

Beginners Only!

Nancy jumped out of bed, forgetting all about the cold. "Maybe it fell off while you were brushing your teeth."

"I looked," George said. "I couldn't find it anywhere."

"Let's look again," Nancy said.

They went into the bathroom and searched. The charm wasn't there.

"When do you remember having it last?" Nancy asked.

George shrugged, then looked under the sink again. "I remember Kelly tying it on in the lodge. After that, I'm not sure."

She stomped back to the bunks and

climbed the ladder to the bed above Nancy's.

"I might as well stay right here for the rest of the weekend." She flopped onto her bed. "I can't ski without my lucky charm."

"Nancy will help you find your silver skis," Bess said. "She can find anything."

"It's no use," George said.

Bess looked at Nancy but didn't say anything else. She climbed into her bunk as Nancy turned off the light.

Nancy lay down in her bed and closed her eyes. She couldn't fall asleep right away. Where could George's necklace be?

"Wake up, sleepyheads!" Nancy's father said the next morning as he poked his head into the girls' room.

The girls got dressed and then went into the kitchen. "Something smells yummy," Bess said. "What is it?"

Nancy sniffed. "I can solve *that* mystery right now," she said. "Pancakes!"

"Case closed, Pumpkin," Mr. Drew said. "It's my special recipe, so dig in."

Nancy noticed that George hardly ate anything. She knew her friend was still upset about losing her necklace.

After breakfast they all headed for the lodge to rent skis. Nancy walked slowly, looking carefully at the path. Maybe George lost her silver skis while we were walking home last night, she thought.

When she didn't see the necklace, Nancy had another idea.

"Can Bess and George and I stop by the game room for a second?" she asked her father. "We want to look for something."

Her father nodded. "Meet me at the ski shop to pick up your boots and skis."

When they got to the game room, Nancy told Bess and George her idea.

"Do you really think it might be here?" George asked.

"There's only one way to find out," Nancy said.

The three friends searched the whole room. The necklace wasn't there.

"I'm sorry, George," Nancy said. "I hope you didn't mean it when you said you wouldn't ski without your necklace."

George shrugged. "I guess I'll ski," she said, trying to smile.

At the ski shop, Mr. Drew and the girls put on their ski boots and picked up their poles and skis. The clerk wrote Nancy's, Bess's, and George's names on pieces of tape and stuck them on each ski.

"This way you'll be able to keep track of whose skis are whose," he told them.

The girls thanked the clerk and followed Mr. Drew out of the shop. It was hard to hold on to everything as they clomped in their heavy ski boots. Bess giggled every time her poles slipped out of her grasp.

"You're supposed to meet the other students over there," Mr. Drew said when they got outside. He pointed to a large group of kids gathered around the ski school instructors. "I'll be skiing on the regular trails. Let's meet back at the lodge for lunch. Have fun!"

The girls hurried to join the group. Bob Murray looked up their names on his list. "Nancy and Bess, you're in Alexandra's Bunny class," he said. He nodded toward a tall woman with blond hair. Several other kids were already standing with her.

"What about me?" George asked eagerly. Nancy was glad George wasn't too worried about her necklace to have fun.

"You're in the Jackrabbit class. Hector is your teacher," Bob Murray said. He pointed at a man with shaggy brown hair, wearing wraparound sunglasses.

"Cool," George said. She grabbed her poles and skis and hurried over to Hector.

Nancy and Bess walked toward Alexandra. "Oh, no. Look who else is in our class," Bess whispered. "It's that grumpy boy from last night."

Nancy saw Will standing next to Al-exandra. "It's cold," he complained.

"Let's just ignore him," Nancy said to Bess.

"We'll start our lesson just as soon as Jennifer arrives," Alexandra told the Bunny group.

Nancy looked around for Jennifer. She saw her talking to Bob Murray. Jennifer put her hands on her hips and shook her head. Finally she turned and walked toward them.

"Is something wrong?" Nancy asked.

"I wanted to be in my sister's class," Jennifer said, looking over at the Jackrabbits.

"But you told us you don't know how to ski," Bess said.

"Kelly says it isn't that hard," Jennifer said. *"You* might not be able to do it, but *I* could."

Jennifer isn't as nice as she was yesterday, Nancy thought.

Alexandra called the Bunny class to attention. She tightened all their boots and showed the students how to put on their skis. "Now we're going to practice walking," she said.

"I *know* how to walk," Jennifer snapped. She took a few steps on her skis, lifting her feet and keeping them straight.

"This is boring," Will complained.

Nancy hoped Jennifer and Will weren't going to be like this all weekend.

Alexandra smiled. "Don't worry, Will, you won't be bored for long."

The Bunny class practiced walking. Then they practiced turning around.

When Will tried to turn, he crossed the tip of one ski over the other. His skis made a big X in the snow.

"I'm stuck!" he cried.

Jennifer rolled her eyes and sighed while Alexandra helped Will get unstuck.

"Now we'll walk sideways up this little hill," Alexandra said after everyone was able to turn around.

Bess giggled as they clomped sideways up the hill. "This isn't so hard."

But when they stopped and looked down the hill, it seemed much bigger and steeper than it had from the bottom.

"Now what?" Bess asked nervously.

"Now we ski down," Alexandra told her.

"I'll break a leg," Will said.

"Keep your knees bent and your weight over the tops of your boots," Alexandra explained. "Like this."

She pushed off with her poles and glided down the hill. "Nancy, you try it," she called when she reached the bottom.

Nancy stuck her poles in the snow and pushed off, just as Alexandra had.

The air rushed past her cheeks. Her skis seemed to fly over the snow. When she reached the flat part at the bottom of the hill, her skis slowed to a stop.

One by one, the rest of the class skied down the hill.

"No problem," Jennifer said. As she reached the bottom, she turned her skis so the tips faced each other.

"Watch out," Will said nervously. "Don't make an X."

"That's how you stop, stupid," Jennifer said. Then she turned to Alexandra. "Now can I switch to Kelly's class? I know how to stop, and no one else in this class does."

"Jennifer just showed us how to stop," Alexandra said to the rest of the class. "It's called making a wedge. Let's all walk up the hill again and try it." She looked at Jennifer. "You, too."

"I'm tired of walking only partway up the slope." Jennifer pointed to the chairs hanging from a cable above them. "When can we ride the ski lift to the top?"

Nancy looked up. She saw George and Kelly sitting in a ski lift chair. It was carrying them to the top of the slope.

"Hector's class is going to ski down part of the trail and meet us at the top of this hill," Alexandra said. "Later we'll take the rope tow up the beginners' slope."

"I thought this *was* the beginners' slope," Bess said.

"It's the *baby* slope," Jennifer said.

Alexandra led the Bunny class back up the small hill. Hector and the Jackrabbits were waiting for them.

"Hi," Nancy said to George. "Are you having fun?"

"Yup," George said. "The only bad thing is those twins are in my class."

Nancy looked and saw Tim and Tom standing in the group of Jackrabbits. One of them saw Nancy looking and crossed his eyes at her.

"I'm glad they're not in our class," Bess whispered. "It's bad enough we have to listen to Will and Jennifer all the time."

"Okay, skiers," Hector called to the two groups. "Line up. We'll go down the hill one at a time."

Nancy was first again. "Good luck," Bess said. She was next in line.

Nancy pushed off and glided down the hill. As she reached the bottom, she aimed the tips of her skis together to make a wedge. It was hard to keep her feet pointed the right way, but she did it. She stopped perfectly and smiled.

Then she heard a scream.

Nancy twisted around, being careful not to cross her skis.

George was speeding down the hill right behind Bess. "Look out, Bess!" George screamed. "I can't stop!"

4

Out of Control

Bess looked over her shoulder. The tips of her skis crossed, and she fell.

George tried to turn, but it was too late. One of her skis went underneath one of Bess's. George tripped and fell right on top of her cousin!

Nancy turned her skis sideways and climbed up the hill toward her friends as fast as she could.

Some of the Bunny and Jackrabbit students waited as Hector and Alexandra skied down the hill toward Bess and George. Kelly, Jennifer, Will, and a few others skied down behind the teachers.

Alexandra and Hector arrived beside Bess and George, tossing up fans of snow as they stopped. Hector helped the girls stand up.

"Are you guys okay?" Nancy cried when she finally reached her friends.

"They're fine," Hector said. "Just a little shaken up."

Then they all skied down to the bottom.

"Who did that?" George asked when they got there. She was covered with snow.

"*You* did," Bess said. She sounded just as cross as her cousin. She was covered with snow, too.

"Okay, girls, settle down. We have to help the others down the hill," Alexandra told them.

"So don't move," Hector said to the group. "We'll be right back."

The two instructors skied off.

"What happened?" Nancy asked when the adults were gone.

George narrowed her eyes. "Someone pushed me," she said.

"That's what everyone says when they fall," Jennifer said. "Right, Kelly?"

Kelly shrugged. "I guess."

Bess dug her ski poles into the snow and straightened up. "If my cousin says she was pushed, she was pushed."

"I told you skiing was stupid," Will said to George.

George ignored him. She still looked angry. "I bet this wouldn't have happened if I still had my good-luck charm."

"Did you lose it?" Jennifer asked.

George nodded.

"That's weird," Kelly said. "You said you couldn't ski without it. And you fell."

"I was *pushed*," George insisted.

By now the rest of the students had reached the bottom of the hill. "Okay, people, time for lunch," Hector said.

"Maybe after lunch George and I should switch classes," Jennifer said to Alexandra. "I didn't fall once."

"No, Jennifer, I don't think so," Alexandra answered.

Nancy and Bess took off their skis.

As they carried them to the ski racks outside the lodge, George walked ahead of them.

Bess leaned close to Nancy. "Poor George. First she loses her silver skis. Then someone pushes her. Why would anyone do that?"

"Maybe they didn't do it on purpose." Nancy frowned. "But then why didn't whoever did it just apologize?"

"Maybe they're chicken. Or creeps like the twins," Bess said. *They* didn't apologize when they almost got ice cream on my sweater last night."

George had leaned her skis against one end of a ski rack right outside the lodge door. "Hurry up," she said. "All that skiing made me hungry."

Nancy and Bess leaned their skis against the rack, too. They looped the straps of their poles over the tips of their skis.

Then they all clomped into the lodge in their ski boots. Nancy liked walking in her ski boots. It was hard, but it made her feel like a real skier.

34

Kelly and Jennifer were standing in the hall outside the dining room. "Are you sure you guys are okay?" Kelly asked George and Bess.

"Yeah," George said. Bess nodded.

"Sometimes when people fall, it scares them," Kelly went on. "It makes it harder for them to ski again."

"I've fallen before," George said. "It's no big deal."

"Kelly, you promised to help me practice," Jennifer said. "We have to hurry. I don't want to have to stay in the baby class *forever*."

The sisters hurried away.

The girls found Nancy's father waiting for them just inside the cafeteria. "How'd it go, girls?" he asked.

"Great," Nancy said.

"Except someone pushed me," George added.

"I bet I know who, too," Bess said. "I think it was—"

Suddenly Bess's voice rose to a shriek. "Tim and Tom!" she cried. "You creeps!"

5

Sticky Skis

One of the twins had snatched Bess's pink ski hat off her head, while the other had jammed his own red stocking cap over Bess's ears.

Bess yanked the stocking cap from her head. "They stole my hat again!"

The twins raced across the hall into the game room. The girls chased them.

"Give that back!" Bess shouted.

"Finders keepers, losers weepers," the first twin said as he jammed Bess's hat onto his head.

Bess reached for her hat. The twin ducked. "Catch me if you can!"

He started to run out of the room.

When he reached the doorway, he bumped into Mr. Drew.

"Oops," the twin said, looking up at Nancy's father.

Just then a woman appeared next to Mr. Drew. "Tom, Tim, did you forget?" she asked. "We're having lunch at the Mountaintop Café today. We're going to ride the gondola."

"Coming, Mom," the twins said at the same time. The first twin took Bess's hat off his head and tossed it toward her. The other twin grabbed the red stocking cap out of her hand.

"Wait," Nancy said to the twins. "Have you seen a silver pendant shaped like skis?"

"Yeah, right." The second twin laughed. "That's girl stuff." Then the boys left the room with their mother.

"Maybe they'll get stuck in a gondola and never come down," George said.

Mr. Drew laughed. "Come on, girls," he said. "Let's have lunch."

Soon they were all back in the cafeteria with steaming plates of food in front of them. "Now, tell me about your latest mystery," Mr. Drew said to Nancy.

"How did you know about the mystery, Daddy?" Nancy asked. She reached for her water glass and took a sip.

Her father smiled. "You aren't the only detective in the family," he said. "I heard you question the twins in the game room just now. And I remembered you were looking for something this morning."

"My necklace," George said. "I lost it last night."

"Don't forget, someone pushed George down the hill," Bess said. "Maybe the same person took her silver skis!"

"Do you think that's what happened, Daddy?" Nancy asked her father.

"You know, Nancy, it's important to get all the facts first," her father said, leaning back in his chair. "Did someone really push George on purpose? Or was it an accident?"

Nancy took a small blue notebook and a pen out of the inside pocket of her ski jacket. It was her mystery note-book. She wrote about all her cases in it.

She turned to a blank page and wrote "The Silver Skis Mystery." Under that she made a list:

1) George's lucky necklace is missing.
2) Someone pushed George down ski slope (on purpose or accident?).

Nancy started a second list. At the top she wrote "Suspects." Then she stopped writing.

"So, who are your suspects?" her father asked, looking at the page.

"The twins, Tim and Tom," Nancy said. "I can't tell them apart, so I guess they're both suspects. And they both could have pushed George." She wrote down the twins' names.

"Why would they do something like that?" Mr. Drew asked.

"They're boys," Bess said. "They don't need a reason to be mean."

Mr. Drew smiled. "Are they your only suspects?"

"What about whiny Will?" Bess asked.

"Well, he was there," Nancy said. "And he hates skiing. So I guess he could have pushed George to try to make the class end earlier." She wrote Will's name down, too.

"Anybody else?" George asked.

"Jennifer and Kelly were nearby when you were pushed," Nancy said.

"Why would they push George?" her father asked.

Nancy thought for a minute. "Jennifer wants to be in the Jackrabbit class instead of the Bunny class," she said.

"She thought the instructors would make us change places if I fell," George said. "She even said so."

"But what about Kelly?" Nancy said. "Would she push George to get Jennifer into the Jackrabbit class?"

"Well, it's a detective's job to find the truth," Mr. Drew said.

"I know," Nancy said. She wrote down the sisters' names. Then she put her notebook away. "We'll have to keep our eyes open for new clues during class this afternoon," she said to her friends.

"Don't worry," George said. "We will!"

After lunch the girls said goodbye to Nancy's father. Then they clomped down the hall toward the door leading outside.

George stopped. "Hey!" she said. "What are my skis doing in here?"

George's skis were leaning against the wall just inside the door.

"Are you sure those are yours?" Nancy asked.

George pointed to the strip of tape with her name written on it. "See? Definitely mine."

"Maybe someone took yours by mistake and left them here," Nancy said.

"Or maybe it was the twins playing another dumb trick," Bess said, looking around. The twins were nowhere in sight.

"Oh, well," George said. "At least my

skis are safe." She picked up her skis and poles and followed Nancy and Bess outside.

Nancy and Bess found their skis where they had left them. The three girls put on their skis. They saw Alexandra and Will standing at the bottom of the beginners' slope. Hector was nearby with Kelly, some of the other Jackrabbits, and Jennifer.

Will waved when he saw Nancy and Bess. "Hurry up. I'm freezing!"

"See you later," George said as she pushed off with her poles.

But she didn't budge.

She pushed again, harder.

Still nothing.

"Something's wrong with my skis," George cried. "I can't move!"

6

Dirty Trick

George took off her skis. She turned them over. The bottoms were covered with lumpy, bumpy ice!

Alexandra skied over to the girls. "What's the problem?" she asked.

George showed the instructor her skis. "Did you leave your skis inside the lodge during lunch?" Alexandra asked.

George shook her head. "No, but someone moved them inside."

"That explains it," Alexandra said. "Your skis got warm inside. When they touched the ground out here, they melted the snow. Since it's so cold out-

44

side, the water refroze. That's why there's ice on the bottom of your skis."

"I can't ski on these," George said. "This is the worst luck ever!"

Hector, Kelly, and Jennifer skied up behind George.

"What happened?" Hector asked.

"George's skis are all iced up," Alexandra said.

"Someone put them inside while we were having lunch," Bess explained.

"Gee, that's too bad," Jennifer said. "I guess you'll have to miss your class, George. But I can take your place."

"That won't be necessary," Alexandra said firmly.

"Right," Hector agreed. "I'll take George to rent another pair of skis." He took off his skis and headed inside with George.

All during class Nancy kept thinking about George's frozen skis. Was this more bad luck? Or was someone out to get George?

By the end of the afternoon, the Bunny class had learned how to use the rope tow and had skied down from a higher part of the mountain. Nancy had a lot of fun. But she still couldn't stop thinking about the mystery.

"I'll see you all at the snowman-building party," Alexandra said when class was over. "There'll be plenty of hot chocolate for everyone."

"I don't like hot chocolate," Will said. "I always burn my tongue."

"Building snowmen is for babies," Jennifer muttered.

"What a couple of party poopers," Bess whispered to Nancy as they went to meet George in the lodge.

The locker room was crowded with Jackrabbits, Bunnies, and kids from the other classes.

"Wow, I'm tired," Bess said as she put on her regular shoes.

"Not me," Jennifer said. "I could ski all day and night."

Jennifer held up her shoes. They were tied together by the shoelaces. She gave one of the laces a quick pull, and they came apart.

"How'd you do that?" Bess asked.

"It's a slip knot," Jennifer said. "Kelly showed me how to do it."

"It's a good trick to know when your fingers are cold," Kelly explained.

"But you have to be careful," Jennifer said. "Or the knot could slip loose when you don't want it to."

Nancy's father was waiting for the girls outside the locker room. "How was skiing this afternoon?" he asked them.

"Okay," George said. "But I bet I would have skied better if I'd had my good-luck charm."

"You would have had better luck, too," Bess said.

Nancy told her father about George's frozen skis.

"That *is* bad luck," he said.

"I think it's another clue," Nancy said. She pulled out her notebook and wrote it down.

Then they headed outside to the snowy field behind the lodge. When they arrived, it was full of people.

"Have fun, girls," Mr. Drew said. "I'm going to get our skis and stuff and take it all back to the apartment. I'll see you in a little while."

"Okay, Daddy," Nancy said.

"Let's build a snow dog," Bess said as Mr. Drew walked away.

"Like Chocolate Chip," George said.

"No fair!" Nancy heard Jennifer shout. Then Jennifer laughed as she scooped up a snowball and threw it at her sister.

Kelly ducked behind the snowman Tim and Tom were building. The snowball hit its head and knocked part of it off.

"Sorry," Jennifer said.

"No problem," one of the twins said. "Tom and I are making a snow monster. It only has one eye anyway."

"And a long monster nose," Tim added. He stuck a stick in the monster's face.

Kelly scooped up another snowball and threw it at Jennifer. It missed her.

"Ow!" Will said. He had just joined

the party and was brushing snow off his coat. "That does it. I'm not building any stupid snowman!" He stomped away.

I guess Will's not having a very good time, Nancy thought. She started to roll a snowball for the snow dog's body.

"Here's a monster nose ring," Nancy heard one of the twins say. She looked up.

One of the boys put something on the snow monster's stick nose.

Nancy's eyes widened. "Where did you get George's necklace?" she shouted.

"Hey!" George cried. She ran to grab her necklace.

But Tom grabbed it first. "Hey, Tim! Catch!" He threw it to his brother.

"Oh, no! Not again," Bess said.

Tim caught the necklace. When George tried to get it, he threw it back to Tom.

But Kelly jumped in and caught it before Tom.

"Good catch, Kelly," George said.

"I'll tie it on for you," Kelly said.

"Tie it tight," George said. "I don't

want to lose it again." She touched the silver charm.

As Kelly tied the ribbon around George's neck, Jennifer giggled. "Better not tie a slip knot, Kelly."

Nancy turned to the twins. "You said you didn't have George's necklace."

"They took it!" Bess shouted.

"We did not," Tom said. "We found it."

Tim pointed to the ground by the side of the lodge. "It was lying in the snow."

Nancy looked where Tim was pointing. There were lots of footprints in the snow—too many to tell who had made them.

How had George's necklace gotten there? she wondered. Someone must have dropped it. Kelly and Jennifer's snowman was nearby. So was the twins' snow monster. And Will had just stomped through there.

Nancy sighed. She had found George's necklace. But the mystery was more mysterious than ever.

7

No Clues

That night after dinner Nancy curled up on her bunk and opened her notebook.

Bess sat down next to Nancy. "I bet the twins moved George's skis today."

George sat down on Nancy's other side. "It couldn't have been the twins," she said. "They had lunch at the Mountaintop Café."

"Maybe they moved them on their way out of the building," Bess argued.

Nancy shook her head. "They were with their mother, remember?"

"Well, they probably took George's necklace," Bess said. "They keep taking my hat."

"Maybe," Nancy said slowly. "But *three* bad-luck things have happened to George. I bet one person did all three." She crossed the twins' names off her suspect list. "That means Tim and Tom couldn't be the ones."

George looked at Nancy's suspect list. "Kelly, Jennifer, and Will were all near me when I was pushed."

Nancy studied her notebook. "Kelly and Jennifer had gone out to practice before the next class," she said. "They could have moved George's skis."

"Will was already waiting for class to begin when we got outside," Bess remembered. "He could have come out early and done it, too."

Nancy looked at the names on her list. Jennifer didn't want to be in the Bunny class. Could she have moved George's skis? Would she have pushed George down the hill just to get into the Jackrabbit class?

Maybe, Nancy thought. But Kelly could have moved the skis and pushed

George, too. Maybe she had done it to help her sister.

"But why would *Will* move your skis, George?" Nancy wondered aloud.

"I don't know," George said. "Maybe he hates skiing so much that he doesn't want anyone else to have fun doing it."

Nancy sighed and closed her notebook. "We still haven't solved the mystery."

George touched her necklace. "But you found my silver skis," she told Nancy. "At least my bad luck is over."

"I hope so," Nancy said. But deep down inside, Nancy had a feeling more bad luck was coming.

Bess looked down at her feet dangling over the edge of the ski lift chair. She quickly leaned back. "Oh, boy. It's a long way down."

The Bunnies had practiced all morning. Now they were riding on the ski lift for the first time.

"This isn't so bad," Nancy heard Will

say to Jennifer. They were in the chair behind Nancy and Bess.

"It's just a chair lift," Jennifer said.

Wow, Nancy thought. Jennifer is cranky about *everything*.

When they reached the top, Nancy and Bess raised the safety bar, stood up on their skis, and slid off the lift. They made a wedge and stopped by Alexandra.

"Everybody ready?" Alexandra said when the whole class was there. "Good. Let's ski!"

"Um, can I *walk* down?" Bess asked.

"You can do it, Bess," Nancy said.

"Just remember not to cross your skis," Will added.

Jennifer pushed her way to the front of the line. "I'll go first. I don't want any of you falling in front of me and making *me* fall."

Alexandra shrugged. "Fine, go ahead."

Jennifer smiled and pushed off down the hill.

When it was her turn, Nancy took a

deep breath and pushed off. She was going so fast! For a moment she was almost afraid. But she had learned a lot this weekend. She turned her skis into a wedge and slowed down. This is fun, she thought.

They practiced skiing down the slope for the rest of the afternoon.

"You all did really well," Alexandra told them when class was over. "Tomorrow morning is the skiing contest. After that there will be an awards ceremony at the Mountaintop Café."

"Thanks for the lessons," Nancy told Alexandra. "They were fun."

"Yeah," Will added. "Skiing isn't as dumb as I thought."

Alexandra smiled. "My pleasure. See you at the skating party by the pond tonight." She pointed to the pond in the distance. "And good luck tomorrow!"

Jennifer dug her poles into the snow and pushed off. "I don't need luck," she said over her shoulder. "Because I'm going to win. And that makes you all losers!"

That night when the girls arrived at the skating party, George quickly put on her skates and hurried off to play ice hockey. Nancy and Bess took their time lacing up their skates.

Nancy noticed Jennifer standing alone by a table with drinks and snacks on it. "Let's set a trap for Jennifer," she whispered to Bess,

"How?" Bess asked.

"If she moved George's skis, that means she knows what they look like, right?" Nancy said.

"That makes sense," Bess agreed.

Nancy stood up. "Come on. I've got a plan." She skated toward Jennifer.

"What plan?" Bess whispered, trying to catch up with her. "What do we do?"

"Just play along," Nancy whispered back. She stopped by the table. "Hi, Jennifer!"

Jennifer had just finished drinking a cup of hot cocoa. "I'm glad you're here,"

Jennifer said. "Kelly's playing ice hockey, and I'm bored. Come skate with me."

"Hey, Jennifer, Bess was thinking about buying some skis," Nancy said as the three girls slowly skated around the pond.

"I was?" Bess said. Nancy elbowed her. "I mean, yes, I was."

"She wants some like the first pair of skis George rented," Nancy continued. "They're good skis. Don't you think so?"

Jennifer shrugged. "I guess. I really didn't notice them."

Nancy studied Jennifer's face. She looked as if she was telling the truth.

The trap hadn't worked very well. Nancy decided to try something else.

"Do you still wish you'd been in the Jackrabbit class?" she asked.

Jennifer laughed. "I was so silly," she said. "If I was in Kelly's class, I'd have to ski against her tomorrow. Kelly's a better skier than I am. But this way, I can win in my class and Kelly can win in hers."

"Someone else might win, you know," Bess said.

Jennifer laughed again. "Now *you're* being silly," she told Bess.

"Jen!" Nancy heard Kelly shout. "Come on. We need another player to win."

"Okay," Jennifer called. "See you later," she said to Nancy and Bess.

Bess glared after her. "That Jennifer thinks she's so great," she said.

"Yes," Nancy said. "And she's still a suspect—even if our trap didn't work."

After breakfast the next morning, Mr. Drew, Nancy, George, and Bess headed for the ski lodge. All three girls were excited about the skiing contest.

They had just reached the front steps when Jennifer came hurrying out. "Hi," she said breathlessly. "We're supposed to meet by the pond this morning instead of the usual place." Then she ran off.

"We'd better hurry," George said. "It's a long walk to the pond."

"I'm going to go find a good place to

watch the action," Mr. Drew said. "Good luck, girls!"

The three friends changed into their ski boots. They carried their skis as fast as they could down the path toward the pond.

"I wonder where everyone is," George said when they arrived.

A woman polishing a snowmobile near an equipment shed looked up. "Are you girls lost?" she asked.

"Isn't this where we're supposed to meet for the skiing contest?" Nancy asked.

The woman shook her head. "The contest is back there." She pointed toward the bottom of the beginners' slope. "It looks as if it's about to start."

George's eyes flashed angrily. "Wait until I find that Jennifer!"

"Come on," Nancy said quickly. "If we run, we might make it."

"We can't run in ski boots!" Bess cried. "We'll never make it in time. It's hopeless!"

8

Winners and Losers

Sounds as if someone played a dirty trick on you," the woman said. "I'll take you over on my snowmobile."

Nancy, Bess, and George put their skis in the sled behind the snowmobile. Then they climbed onto the snowmobile seat. A moment later they were zooming back toward the slope.

"Thanks," Nancy said when the snowmobile came to a stop. She jumped off, grabbed her skis, and raced toward Alexandra. Bess was right behind her.

George rushed past them to the lift. The rest of the Jackrabbit class was already riding up the hill.

"You're late," Alexandra said. She was frowning.

"It wasn't our fault," Bess said. "Someone told us to go to the pond." She glared at Jennifer. But Jennifer wouldn't look at her.

Nancy and Bess put on their skis and got on the ski lift. As they rode to the top of the hill, they saw George skiing down. Nancy thought she skied well.

Kelly skied down a moment later. She's good, too, Nancy thought. Almost as good as those skiers in the videos.

Finally they reached the top, and it was time for the Bunny class to ski.

Will fell halfway down the hill, then slid the rest of the way to the bottom. But when he got up, he was laughing.

Then Jennifer dug her ski poles into the snow and pushed off hard—so hard she fell right over the front of her skis! She stood up and pushed off again. This time she finished the course perfectly.

"That was brave of her," Nancy said. "She didn't quit just because she fell."

"She's still a sneak," Bess said.

Nancy was next. She took a deep breath and pushed off. The wind rushed past her. She pointed her skis into a wedge and zigzagged down the snowy trail.

"That was great!" George said when Nancy reached the bottom of the hill.

"Thanks," Nancy said. "You were great, too." She glanced over at the people watching and saw her father waving at her and grinning proudly.

Nancy and George watched as Bess skied down the hill. Bess went very, very slowly. But she didn't fall once.

Nancy and George cheered as Bess crossed the finish line.

"I *knew* it was Jennifer!" Bess crowed at lunch. "Her mean trick almost made us miss the contest. That proves it!"

Nancy reached for her notebook. She crossed off Will's name. He liked skiing now, so he wasn't a suspect anymore.

That left Jennifer and Kelly. And

Jennifer had lied to them about meeting at the pond. That meant she must be the one.

Something isn't right, Nancy thought, putting her notebook away. But she wasn't sure what was bothering her.

Nancy was still thinking about the mystery that afternoon as they got ready to go to the awards ceremony.

"Why would she do it?" Nancy muttered under her breath on the way to the gondola lift.

"What?" George asked.

"We thought Jennifer did everything because she wanted to be a Jackrabbit," Nancy said. "But then she decided she didn't. So why would she *keep* doing mean things to you, George? It doesn't make sense. Unless . . ."

Nancy saw George reknot the velvet ribbon of her necklace. The silver skis caught the late-afternoon sun and flashed brightly.

Just then Nancy remembered that Kelly knew how to tie a slip knot. And Jennifer had told a joke about Kelly tying George's necklace on with a slip knot, too.

"That's it!" Nancy said. She looked ahead at the gondola line, then turned to her father. "Can we ride the gondola with our friends?"

When he nodded, Nancy grabbed George and Bess. She pushed through the line until they were standing with Kelly, Jennifer, and their parents.

When the next gondola came, Nancy led George and Bess onto it, right behind the sisters. The gondola was full.

"You'll have to catch the next one," the gondola operator told Kelly and Jennifer's parents.

The gondola lifted them higher and higher up the side of the mountain.

Nancy faced Kelly and Jennifer. "Kelly, I know you're the one who's been doing mean things to George."

Kelly shrugged and stared out the window. "I don't know what you're talking about."

Nancy looked at Jennifer. "Kelly

67

made you tell us to go to the pond, didn't she?"

Jennifer glanced at Kelly. "No," she said. "I really thought we were meeting there."

Nancy wasn't going to give up. She moved closer to Jennifer. "Kelly *told* you that, right? We know, because we know it was Kelly who stole George's good-luck charm and pushed her down the hill."

"You can't prove that," Kelly burst out. "Anyway, what makes you think I took her stupid necklace?"

"The slip knot," Nancy said. "You used that kind of knot on George's necklace. Am I right?"

For a minute it looked as though Kelly was going to deny it. Then she glanced at her sister and sighed. "Yes," she told Nancy quietly. "I tied the ribbon with a very loose slip knot so it would come off. I saw it fall outside the lodge and I picked it up."

"Then you dropped it by accident and the twins found it," Nancy said.

Kelly nodded. "That's right. I did all the other things, too."

"Why?" George demanded.

Kelly met George's eyes. "Last year at the contest I fell and didn't finish. Everyone laughed at me. I wanted to win this year. No one laughs at a winner."

The gondola bumped to a stop at the top of the mountain. Kelly jumped out and started running.

Jennifer got out, too. "I'm sorry," she said. Then she ran after her sister.

The Mountaintop Café was buzzing with excitement as Alexandra announced the award winners in the Bunny class.

Bess won an award for being the skier with the most style. Will won for having the most improved attitude.

Even Jennifer won an award. It was for being the bravest skier—because she finished the contest after she had fallen.

"Finally, the award you've all been waiting for," Alexandra announced.

"For the best overall skier in the Bunny group, our award goes to Nancy Drew."

Nancy smiled proudly as she shook Alexandra's hand.

Nancy noticed that everyone in the class had received an award. No one was a loser.

But she couldn't help holding her breath when it was time to announce the awards for the Jackrabbit class.

"Everyone worked hard," Hector said. "But we think the most promising skier is Georgia Fayne."

George made a face at hearing her whole name. But she grinned as she went to get her award.

Tim and Tom got awards for being the fastest twins on skis. They ran up to get their awards and ran back to their seats.

"And the best all-around skier in the Jackrabbit class is Kelly Allen."

Nancy clapped politely as Kelly got her award. Bess didn't clap.

As Kelly walked by their table back to her own, George jumped up and stuck out her hand. "Congratulations, Kelly."

"You mean it?" Kelly said.

"Sure," George said. "Even though you tried to cheat, you won the contest fair and square. You *were* the best skier."

Kelly shook George's hand. Then, in a low voice, she said, "I'm really sorry, George."

"It's okay," George said. She grinned. "Just don't try anything like that next year!"

That evening Nancy finished packing before Bess and George. She took out her notebook and sat on her bunk.

She turned to the page headed "The Silver Skis Mystery." At the bottom she wrote:

I learned to ski this weekend, and I won a prize for it. I solved a mystery, too. When I solved the

71

mystery, I learned something important. Winning is fun, but not if all you care about is winning. And if you have to cheat to win, you haven't really won at all.

Case closed.

TAKE A RIDE
WITH THE KIDS ON BUS FIVE!

Natalie Adams and James Penny have just started
third grade. They like their teacher, and they like
Maple Street School. The only trouble is, they have
to ride bad old Bus Five to get there!

#1 THE BAD NEWS BULLY
Can Natalie and James stop the bully on Bus Five?

#2 WILD MAN AT THE WHEEL
When Mr. Balter calls in sick,
the kids get some strange new drivers.

#3 FINDERS KEEPERS
The kids on Bus Five keep losing things.
Is there a thief on board?

(And coming soon)
#4 I SURVIVED ON BUS FIVE
Bad luck turns into big fun
when Bus Five breaks down in a rainstorm.

BY MARCIA LEONARD
ILLUSTRATED BY JULIE DURRELL

A MINSTREL® BOOK
Published by Pocket Books

1237-03

FULL HOUSE™
Michelle

#1: THE GREAT PET PROJECT 51905-0/$3.50

#2: THE SUPER-DUPER SLEEPOVER PARTY
51906-9/$3.50

#3: MY TWO BEST FRIENDS 52271-X/$3.50

#4: LUCKY, LUCKY DAY 52272-8/$3.50

#5: THE GHOST IN MY CLOSET 53573-0/$3.99

#6: BALLET SURPRISE 53574-9/$3.99

#7: MAJOR LEAGUE TROUBLE 53575-7/$3.50

#8: MY FOURTH-GRADE MESS 53576-5/$3.99

#9: BUNK 3, TEDDY, AND ME 56834-5/$3.50

#10: MY BEST FRIEND IS A MOVIE STAR!
(Super Edition) 56835-3/$3.50

#11: THE BIG TURKEY ESCAPE 56836-1/$3.50

#12: THE SUBSTITUTE TEACHER 00364-X/$3.50

A MINSTREL® BOOK

Published by Pocket Books

Simon & Schuster Mail Order Dept. BWB
200 Old Tappan Rd., Old Tappan, N.J. 07675

Please send me the books I have checked above. I am enclosing $_____(please add $0.75 to cover the postage and handling for each order. Please add appropriate sales tax). Send check or money order--no cash or C.O.D.'s please. Allow up to six weeks for delivery. For purchase over $10.00 you may use VISA: card number, expiration date and customer signature must be included.

Name _____

Address _____

City _____ State/Zip _____

VISA Card # _____ Exp.Date _____

Signature _____

1033-15